IN THE LINE
OF DESTINY

By SRIRAM B.

COPYRIGHT

DISCLAIMER

This is a work of fiction. Names, characters, businesses, places, events and incidents are either the products of the author's imagination or used in a fictitious manner. Any resemblance to actual persons, living or dead, or actual events is purely coincidental.

Dedicated to:

My three children

My Love - My Life - My
Inspiration

Chapter One

Looking through the taxi window the skyline of Kuala Lumpur gleamed with all its exotic appeal. Winding through the narrow streets the taxi finally came to a halt, 40 ringgits signal the driver. The man in the back seat handed out the cash and jumped out of the cab heading into a dingy apartment complex.

Climbing the stairs to the second floor he quickly opened the door and stepped into the apartment, placing the plastic bag he carried with him from the shopping trip. He dragged a chair to the center of the living room and pulled out a rope from the bag, carrying it over his head he looped the rope into the ring in the ceiling. So convenient he thought to himself it's just the thing I needed. He pulled the rope down and created a noose trying it on for the right fit he adjusted the rope stepping back, he imagined how it would look hanging from the ceiling. He then walked over to the window and stared out; it was a beautiful day. How on earth did I do this to myself he wondered.

Chapter Two

Glancing at the watch he arranged his clothes and spent time grooming himself. He wanted to die looking at his best as that was the least, he could do. Sitting down at the writing-table he wrote a letter to the local authorities it read:

To the Local Authorities - Bangkok

No one is to be held responsible for my death. I have simply lost hope and have nothing to live. My passport and travel documents are in the writing-table draw.

He folded the letter and placed a paperweight on it. It was time, he thought getting onto the chair and pulling the noose tight. His neck hurt but it was nothing compared to what he had been through. Finally, the time had come. I would you have preferred to leave on a better note he signed and lifted his leg to kick the chair when the phone buzzed. Glancing down he could see it vibrating violently on the table, this is the last thing I need he thought when a dark figure appeared at the corner of the room. Surprised and completely in shock he pulled the rope off his neck and stepped back onto the floor but the figure was gone. It was a shadow from the tree outside. Damn, he thought I have to go through this again. The phone rang again, who the hell is this he thought picking it up. The number was from Muscat, a city in Oman situated in the Middle East. The voice on the other end inquired "is this Sam MacDonald?" Yes. "This is Mariam from the TechnoTSP group of companies. We are headquartered in Muscat and you have been selected for a job interview with our MD today". "But I never applied" quipped Sam. "You were referred by a client of yours, the MD will fill you in". "Can I schedule it for 30 minutes from now"? "Okay," said Sam "I will be waiting, and thanks for the call". Hanging up Sam sat on the couch wondering what a bummer, now I have a job interview before I hang myself. Anyways one last hoorah before I go, should have asked for the MD's name and the job role he thought when his eyes fell on something glittering on the floor. It was a ring with a honey-colored stone crafted in silver.

Chapter Three

Wonder who it belongs to? Must have been from the previous guests assumed Sam, I will return it to the helpdesk when I get a chance but something in him coaxed him to try it on. It was a perfect fit for the ring finger where the lines of the engagement ring remained. At that very moment, the phone rang it was from the MD. "Hello," said Sam unsure as to what to expect. "Hi, I am Ali Razak the MD at TechnoTSP Muscat. I was given your reference from MGCB Engineers who are based in Qatar. I believe you were the one who installed the ERP system and they are very happy with your support and product knowledge. We are looking to develop an ERP system ground up and we are looking for a technical consultant to help get the workflow and functionality in place. I believe you are the right guy for the job, so when can you join us?" This was the last thing Sam expected as it was a job offer on a platter. "I can be there in a week" managed Sam. " I am currently in Kuala Lumpur on a holiday". "That is great I'm sure you're wondering about the package. We will offer a 20% hike on your current package and will provide you with accommodation and a car. The project will be for three years and after that, we can revise your role. My secretary will get in touch with you to get the contract signed and arrange for your travel and visa arrangements. We're happy to have you on board". There was a silence on the other side and Sam managed to thank Ali profusely before hanging up. Dumbstruck, Sam could not believe what had just happened. That was not an interview, the job offer was given without uttering a single word on his experience and education. The salary and perks were amazing and the job role was a dream come true. Sam had always envisioned being part of the development team and R&D department. Now it was all going to happen as he was just about to hang himself. What timing, he thought just a minute off and he would have missed the opportunity of a lifetime. Muscat, I wonder if there would be any problems on arrival. Would I be arrested and put behind bars or deported? Was this a mistake, could this be a trap?

Chapter Four

The phone rang again. "Hi, I am the secretary of Mr.Razaq. My name is Alia and I am calling to arrange your visa and air tickets. Can you please mail me your passport copy and highest qualification certificate to apply for your visa? Once you are here a medical will be done and your residence visa will be stamped on the passport. Can I book your tickets for a week from now, that would be the 14th of October"? "That's ok," said Sam. Still in utter shock and the speed at which things were moving forward. "Can I have your email and alternative contact number, please"? She noted it down and hung up. A minute later a welcome mail arrived at the inbox requesting a copy of Sam's documents. He emailed the documents and sat back to wonder the turn life had taken in an hour. Everything in life seemed lost and now he was on his way to an exotic unknown land with an amazing job offer and a salary he could only dream of achieving. A second mail arrived with a salary advance request. Sam replied with his bank account details and a few minutes later the approval arrived.

Unbelievable thought Sam. Should I inform Kathy he contemplated. It is too early, let me first get to Muscat and if all is well I can contact her. It's not like she cares. Another mail with the job contract was attached for his perusal and signature. Sam browsed through it in utter excitement, this is not a trap it's happening. He quickly signed the documents digitally and sent them out. A few minutes later the salary advanced transfer receipt arrived, it was three months' salary in advance to help Sam settle down. It was all too much and Sam was left numb with the developments. He was suddenly broken out of the trance with a knock on the door. He hurriedly removed the rope from the ceiling and answered the door. It was the room keeper. "Sir, I'm sorry to disturb you but the previous guest had called us and is looking for a ring that he has misplaced. Can I have a look if you don't mind?" "Sure," said Sam. "In fact", but he stopped his words before they got out and quickly inserted his hands into his pant pocket.

Chapter Five

"I have checked the floor but no signs of the ring if you do find it in any of the cupboards please drop it off at the reception. We are sorry for the inconvenience but the customer was very insistent we search". No problem muttered Sam I will also keep an eye out for it and will let you know if I get it". Closing the door behind him Sam was ashamed, that was cheap on my part to lie but then there was a voice within that asked him to hold onto it. Could there be a connection between the ring and his sudden turn in fortune? Anyways only time will tell. A message appeared on his phone, the salary advance was credited to his account. Wow yelled Sam. I have not seen so much money in my account in a long time, he hastily took a screenshot and admired it. All those years of working hard and the screenshot were the only achievement to show for shameful thoughts, Sam. Turning around to see a black figure standing at the corner of the room, ah the shadow again thought Sam but something was not right. It was moving and as Sam stared in disbelief he found himself face to face with a cloaked figure.

Chapter Six

Sam was motionless as the dark figure moved closer. It was made up of black and grey smoke with minute red amber's flashing inside the cloud of smoke. It was a cloud that took the shape of a cloaked figure. Sam tried hard not to pass out as his heart rate increased drastically. His mind was racing and he desperately wanted to scream for help but his voice froze and could hardly utter a word. He was horrified but then the dark figure puts his hand out signaling to stay calm, It had no intention of hurting him. Stepping closer it pointed to the ring he wore, the one he had lied about. Sam tried hard to look and identify a face under the cloud but it was just a dark mass of grey and black with no features, it was like staring into the night sky with no stars or moon to provide the light. A grey smog with no end in sight. The figure formed a hand, it pointed to his ring finger on the left hand. "Do you want the ring?" Sam shouted "You can have it" he hastily pulled it out and offered but the figure indicated the opposite. It wanted him to wear the ring on the right-hand ring finger instead of the left. As Sam slipped the ring into his finger the figure vanished.

Chapter Seven

Sam stumbled back and collapsed on the sofa, he was sweating profusely as the fear passed through his every cell. His first reaction was to bolt out of the door and vacate the apartment but sanity prevailed. The dark figure did not want to hurt him but was trying to tell him something about the ring he had heard stories of objects being haunted or possessed with spirits and wondered if this was the case. He was in two minds about his newfound fortune and luck which was forcing him to create a connection between the ring and the current situation. What if everything goes back to normal the state of hopelessness and agony he had found himself in over the past few years. The drudgery of daily unrewarding motion of life that he had endured for so long. He had longed for a light at the end of the tunnel and now was in the open. Life had given him a second chance, Sam was starting to hope again and the dreams of a better life were creeping in. He felt motivated and wanted to achieve success and amass a fortune contrary to hanging himself in a foreign land. Can the past be undone? If life can throw all the worst people, experiences, and financial situations, it can also give you the best of people, friends, family, and success. If one can be poor, homeless, Bankrupt, and abandoned the opposite also exists under the same sky. So why cannot my life turn a leaf, what if I could pick myself up from here on and soar to the highest potential? This is what I felt when I got out of college but then Events had turned out just the opposite. 10 years down the line he found himself penniless, hopeless, and not a glimmer of positivity. His passion to travel, enjoy the fine things in life was all but a distant dream, which he was scared to face. Over time the dreams faded and pure sustenance and survival became the only aim. There was no forward momentum only trying desperately to hold on from the inevitable fall into the abyss with no end in sight. The ring had changed all that in a matter of hours. He was a changed person, the passion to live and achieve had returned. He was raring to get back on the trail but the doubts crawled in, what if this was just a coincidence? The luck must be tested and verified.

Chapter Eight

Genting island off the coast of Kuala Lumpur dedicated only to the gambling industry. Heaven for gamblers with wonderful resorts catering to the needs and wants of people who want to put their luck to the test.

Arriving at the island Sam pulled out 2000 ringgits from the ATM and strolled on the streets as the crowd hastily moved in and out of the resorts and clubs. It was the Last Vegas of the east. Sam decided to enter the sky island east resort, it was an oriental style building with two foo dogs guarding the entrance. The mythical creature was believed to protect the establishment from thieves and loss of money. A huge Bagua adorned the building entrance to protect the patrons from negative energy. The interior had symbols of money in the form of ancient copper coins embedded in the walls and ceiling. There were gold ingots placed in a heap in the centre and a wealth jar overflowing with rice and money, the symbol of wealth and accumulation of assets. The decor was a blend of red and gold. The senses were bombarded with various wealth-related symbols and artefacts stimulating the mind to gamble and create wealth unfortunately not many are successful and the establishment always wins.

As Sam entered he was greeted at the reception by two beautiful women dressed in mini skirts and tank tops. They ushered him into the reception where another lady took down his details. "Passport please". After scanning his documents they offered him a form which was a self-declaration to take all responsibilities for the loss of money and the establishment was not to be blamed for any incidents. Sam signed it and exchange the 2000 ringgits for 20 chips of 100. "Another thousand Ringgits and you get two chips on the house" she tempted him. The two women next to him nudged and it was enough for Sam to pull out his wallet and offer his card for a swipe of another 1000. He knew they had taken him for a ride but he was helpless, such are the effects of the woman who are a catalyst to open your wallet. They were going about their jobs amazingly well as Sam saw another helpless gentleman pull out 20,000 ringgits.

At this point, the two women departed and he was joined by another lady. She wore high heels and was clothed in hot pants, a sleeveless top that was unbuttoned. "This was this way Sir" she led him through a huge arch to enter the play zone. It was a two-storied gamblers paradise, drinks were on the house and the resort offered accommodation for clients who spent more than 50,000 ringgits in a day. "Drinks"? offered by the Hostess but Sam reluctantly declined as he wanted to stay sharp for the game ahead. "So what is your poison"? she inquired with a smile waving her hand. "Three Cards," said Sam pointing to the middle of the parlour. Six tables were set up with four players on each. The dealer dealt 3 cards to each at the table and the highest set of cards won. It was a high stakes game and one that purely was based on luck as the player cannot see the cards. Once they decide to see the cards and play on, the stakes were doubled for the player where the others were still on the same bet. Sam sat down at the table with three gentlemen. Amit for Singapore, Tai from Indonesia and Jeff from America. They signalled to the dealer to start dealing with the cards.

Chapter Nine

The dealer shuffled the cards and dealt three cards each. "Starting bets please," said the Dealer. The players placed one coin in the center of the table. Sam placed another coin so did the others. The blind bets went on for four rounds, till Amit looked at his cards and folded. Jeff followed, only Sam and Tai remained. Sam dropped down two more coins and increased the stakes. Tai followed and they went on for five rounds. Sam had put down 15 coins, which was equal to 1500 ringgits. Finally, Tai dropped four coins and asked for a show. Sam gingerly opened his cards and it was two Aces and one King. Tai opened his first card which was an Ace of Heart the second was a King of heart, now the only card that could beat Sam was a Queen or another card with hearts. It was a two of diamond. Tai let a grunt of frustration and wrapped his hands on the table. Sam was up, he had more than doubled his money within fifteen minutes. The next round took a similar route with Sam winning in the end. Three games had passed and Sam was unstoppable, he had won with the lowest combinations and he was Jubilant. "Drinks for everyone on the table" he announced proudly. Sipping on whiskey he was eager to move on but the other players were reluctant. They were forced to rejoin as the other tables were occupied. Two drinks down and into the fourth game, Amit was conservative and folded after three rounds of the start. Jeff held on till the 7th round and finally looked at his cards, he too folded. The game went on for 20 rounds as Sam was confident it was his night and Tai had only four coins left. He desperately put them down and asked for a show. Sam turned his first card and it was a two of hearts, the second a queen of diamond and the third Ace of spades. Tai had a straight flush, king, Queen, and Jack. It was a sudden turn of events against the flow of luck. Three more games followed and Sam was at the losing end, he had only six coins left and on the eighth game exited with a set of bad cards. It was an unbelievable turn of fortune, the three men at the table gleamed as Sam withdrew from the table.

I should have got out when I was winning, just got carried away with the good run and have been more careful, cursed Sam. Guess the ring is not lucky after all, I have lost all my money. It just inflated my ego and brought me down crashing to the ground.

Chapter Ten

Sam hopped into the ATM and pulled out 1000 ringgits and stopped by a café to catch up on dinner. He ordered a bowl of noodles and wok-fried chicken. It had been a long time since he had visited a restaurant. The financial constraints of the past few months had put him on a strict leash. He was eating home-cooked meals and was only able to afford a restaurant meal once a month. Now he was all by himself the dream left behind and the zest for living in the moment a distant thought. All the years of reading management books had yielded no results when it mattered and despite his sincere efforts found himself penniless, jobless, and alone.

The people he had helped and supported had deserted him in the time of need, the ones he trusted had turned their back on him. Put to the test none stood up and the whole support system one depends on in time of crisis just wasn't there and none of them were apologetic nor care to explain themselves. It was a rude awakening unfortunately it came at a crucial time, a point of no return.

I should have pulled those strings earlier, tested the strength of the relationships cursed Sam. I would have never landed myself in this position.

One can accept a mistake that is committed by self but it is an understatement of the debacle that brought me to my knees by the mistakes of others. How do you get over being cheated, exploited, lied to, abandoned, and humiliated for the faults of others? It still gave him a shudder thinking about the past year but now there was a glimmer of hope which had been trashed to bits.

The last hope of resurrecting his life had fallen flat on the face. Sam was desperately clutching the straws of hope and now the downfall in his spirit was inevitable. As he swallowed the noodles his demoir changed, a feeling of positivity came over him. A voice inside him urged him to pick the pieces. Not all is lost, one must change and be mentally strong. No one cares so you owe it to yourself to get out of this deep pit and succeed. Not for others but for yourself, to prove what you can achieve.

Chapter Eleven

It was close to 2:00 AM when Sam walked back into the Casino. He walked directly over to the table to the utter amusement of the players, waited patiently as a game was in progress till one of the players left the table. "So you're back with more cash to lose" giggled Jeff. "Hope you have enough to last the night," said Sam while instructing the dealer to proceed. "Bets please," said the Dealer. "I am placing a starting bet of 500 ringgits" announced Sam. The group of men looked at each other and then went on to place their bets. Amit raised the stakes to 1000 ringgits per round. Sam to their surprise tossed the coins. "You have come prepared," said Tai putting down his bet. The next round went on for 2000 ringgits, it was getting nervous as Amit picked up the cards and folded. Jeff did the same. I will raise the stakes to 3000 ringgits said the Tai. Sam countered with the same and Tai looked at his cards to continue at double the bet.

By now a small crowd had gathered around the table. It was a matter of courage and wits, Sam remained blind and placed another 3000 ringgits. Tai put down 6000 ringgits as Sam signaled the dealer for a credit line. "How much?" said the dealer, "till the gentleman opposite to me folds," said Sam smiling and handing over his debit card. The dealer swiped and took a sum of 10000 ringgits and handed the chips to Sam. Tai smiled and raised his bets to 10,000 ringgits. Sam put down 5000 ringgits and asked Tai to play. It was an unexpected move as Tai had to cough up 10,000 ringgits and an additional 20000 ringgits for a show. He was already down by 27,500 ringgits, if Tai folded he would lose all his money, if he played he had to cough up another 10,000 ringgits. What if Sam's cards were better? But he was still blind which meant the cards could be worse. Tai's cards were strong but could he risk 30000 over it? Finally, he succumbed to the pressure of the crowd and the beautiful women around him by placing the amount on the table and asking for a show.

There were 87,000 ringgits on the table to win and the suspense had reached boiling point. Sam opened the first card and it was an Ace of Spades the second was a meagre Four of Spades. Now for the final card, Sam looked up and saw Tai smile. As Sam was about to turn the last card Tai picked his first card, it was a King of Diamonds. The second was an Ace of Clover. He went on to flip his third card which was a King of Hearts. Tai had two Kings which was hard to beat. It was a strong hand and only two combinations could beat him, a full set of the same color cards or a double Ace. It was the moment of truth, Sam turned the card around as the crowd screamed in excitement and jumped out of their seats. It was Ace of Hearts. Tai was devastated and walked away while the crowd gathered around Sam to congratulate him. He had come away with 87,000 ringgits in the most dramatic fashion, fortune favors the brave.

Chapter Twelve

Sam collected his winnings from the counter and stepped out of the casino when someone placed a hand on his shoulder, turning around it was Amit from the table. My name is Amit I am based out of Singapore. Sam re-introduced himself. That was an impressive game, what made you come back? Inquired Amit. "I was desperate to win, just wanted something positive to cling on to" answered Sam. I run a software company in India but we have offices in the USA and Singapore. I manage the Singapore branch and am in charge of new product development. We have an old solution that needs to be recoded and new features added. Since you're a software analyst would you be interested to work on this project? Sam was surprised at the sudden opportunity which had presented itself. "I have just signed up for a three-year contract in Muscat and am waiting for my visa". "You can work as a consultant, we will pay handsomely and you can work remotely. You may have to come in once a month just to test the product and guide the developers". Said Amit. "have to think about it, not sure I will have the time to do both jobs," said Sam. "Let's do one thing," said Amit pointing at the bar. "Give it a shot for two months and if it goes as per plan we can cancel the deal". Sam gave it a good thought and agreed. Amit gave him his visiting card and asked him to email Sam CV and bank account details for transferring the consulting fees along with the passport copy.

It was a great day and Sam wanted to celebrate he invited Amit for drinks and walked into the bar which was still open. It was 5:00 AM when Sam caught a taxi and returned to the apartment. He plonked on the bed and woke up a good 10 hours later. Gingerly walking over to the pantry area he reached out for a glass of milk to soothe the hangover. He recollected the events of the previous night and dwelled in the emotion of winning and succeeding after years of banging on the door.

He had finally found the key to open the door to success, fame, and wealth. Opportunity to make wealth was pouring in and it was a stark contrast to where he was a few days ago. Drained of energy, luck, and most importantly opportunity, devoid of which there was no starting point and it was a slow agonizing fall from grace. Let me contact Amit thought Sam reaching out for his wallet but it was not to be found. He looked around the apartment but there was no sign of it.

Chapter Thirteen

Sam went over the entire apartment but his wallet was missing, It had the winnings of last night. I must have left it in the cab thought Sam as his eyes fell upon the table, the laptop was missing too. Alarmed Sam opened the writing-table draw to find It empty. He had been robbed, his laptop, phone wallet, and passport were all missing. Sam was now stranded with no money. It was now evident the wallet was not misplaced in the taxi, how and who could have done this? Sam ran over to the reception area to explain what had happened and requested them to go through the CCTV footage. The manager pulled a chair and ask them to sit down as he scanned the day's footage. "Any idea when you came over"? "Must have been around 5:00 AM". Fast-forwarding the video to 5:00 AM they saw Sam being carried into the apartment by two men they were wearing caps so their faces were hidden but Sam recollected the shirts. It was Amit and Jeff from the Casino. They had tricked him into having a drink and had robbed him.

They had cleaned the place up leaving no evidence, the visiting card Amit gave him must have been a fake. They have been working in a group all along to rob players who left the casino after winning. 30 minutes later the two were seen leaving the apartment.

 Sam called the local police and informed them of the crime and passed on his contact details. He also emailed them a copy of the video and requested them to check with the casino to match the CCTV footage. It was a rollercoaster of a day with the highs and the low. One minute Sam was in disbelief as to how his life had changed and here he was in complete dismay, losing everything he had.

His trip to Muscat was now in jeopardy without a passport. A duplicate could take months, without his laptop and phone Sam did not have his bank account details and credit card numbers to make a complaint. What have I done to deserve this, I even gave the Asian 10,000 ringgits when he was sobbing on the street. Wait a second thought Sam when did I do that? It was a vague memory but he remembered stepping out of the bar and finding Tai sobbing on the street, it had been a hard blow, and all his earnings we lost. He had nothing left to take care of his family back in Indonesia. Sam could understand this pain of being penniless and no one to depend on so he gave him 10,000 ringgits and told him to take care of his family.

Chapter Fourteen

With no money, Sam had no choice but to stay in the apartment. Boredom was catching up and he finally fell asleep. He was woken by the doorbell which shrilled through the apartment. Opening the door the manager held out a cordless phone, "it is from the police". "Yes" answered Sam. The constable on the other end of the line asked him to come over to the main police station situated at Jurong. He hung up before Sam could ask any further questions. Embarrassed he asked the manager for some cash to take a bus to the station. The manager gave him 100 ringgits, Sam took a bus and walked the remaining distance to the police station.

On arrival he was greeted by Sergeant Lim, he asked him to sit down while he walked over to the table and picked up a box. I believe these are your belongings? Inside was Sam's laptop, phone, passport, and wallet alongside it was a bundle of money and the winning ticket. "Thank you," said Sam with a great sense of relief. "How did you get it"? "Well, we checked the CCTV footage you sent and compared them with the casino, we sent out a lookout at all major stations, bus stops, airports terminals, and land borders. The two men tried crossing over to Singapore using the land border and were caught. We believe they are a gang of con artists who cheat and rob visitors to the country. They have been interrogated and have confessed to robbing you after you left the casino. Please count your cash and belongings and do let us know if anything is missing. Once you sign the records you cannot demand or file another case in case something is missing".

 Sam went through his belongings and everything was there, he went on to count the cash and there were 87,000 ringgits the amount he had won, and 2000 ringgits which had been withdrawn from the ATM. "We found the cash on them and going by your statements we have kept the winning receipt and the amount you had withdrawn from the ATM". Sam thanked the officials and signed the documents and left the station.

He hailed a taxi and returned to the apartment relieved and his faith restored in his newfound luck. Returning the 100 ringgits to the manager he explained what had happened and thanked him for his help. Back in the apartment, Sam jumped with joy that was a close call and life had taken a 180-degree turn. He was glad it had worked out as the alternative was a nightmare even to think about. suddenly it occurred to

Sam they were supposed to be only 77,000 ringgits as he had given 10,000 to Tai but had gotten it back in a mysterious way.

Chapter Fifteen

Sam woke up the next morning to the sound of his mobile phone. It was from Muscat, Alia's voice sounded excited, "Sam we have received your visa, can I book your tickets for the coming Wednesday as Friday and Saturday is the weekend in these parts". "Okay," said Sam. "Where will I be staying"? "We will book you in a hotel for two weeks within which you can finalize accommodation for yourself. Once the visa formalities are done you can sponsor your wife and kids. The company will pay for the expenses of course". "I am single said Sam with a sense of sadness". "I will mail you the tickets, please carry a copy of the visa, and once you reach immigration exchange it for the original which shall be deposited at the airport". "OK, thank you" said Sam. "See you in Muscat".

30 minutes later the tickets were in the email, it was a business class ticket with a stopover at Delhi airport. Sam took a stroll to the nearest money exchange and sent ringgit 60,000 towards his credit card dues. As Sam stepped out he saw the dark figure on the opposite side of the road. The figure stood there looking at Sam then disappeared. When Sam returned to the apartment he received an SMS message. An amount of 120,000 ringgits had been credited

to the account from his previous employer, it was his final settlement which had been delayed for over 8 months. What is happening? Thought Sam, one moment I was bankrupt and ready to hang myself. The last few months had robbed him of his money, job, status, and relationships? Everything that went gone wrong had no logical explanation except a steady stream of bad luck and financial constraints, which ultimately left Sam penniless and with no means to generate revenue or upkeep his basic needs.

Now it was just the opposite, a daily incremental dose of good luck this was proof if poverty and bad luck existed the other side of the coin was good luck, wealth, abundance, and prosperity but what defines which side you land? Was it your luck, hard work or just being at the right place at the right time?. How are millionaires made and paupers created? Sam had worked hard, done all the right things, created no enemies, helped everyone he could but found himself in utter misery and poverty for doing all the right things. He only bore the wrath of life in return.

Chapter Sixteen

Muscat was a city popular in the Middle Ages for the frankincense trade. Situated in the Middle East bordering UAE and Saudi Arabia it is one of the bustling ports and cities in the Arabian Peninsula.

Sam walked out of the airport to be greeted by a tall chap who looked to be of African descent. "Hello" Mr. Sam. I am Abdul the personal relationships officer. I was sent to pick you up and drop you off at the hotel". Abdul quickly took Sam's suitcase and ushered him over to a minivan, loaded it, and sped towards the city.

 Abdul handed Sam a set of keys to Sam's amusement. "This is for your car, it is parked at the hotel. I assume you have an international driving license"? "Yes" confirmed Sam. "You will meet with Mr. Arif in the morning, I have sent you the details of the location on your phone, just use the GPS".

On arrival at the hotel, Abdul requested Sam for his passport which he checked and handed over to the front desk. The Arabian Inn Peridot was a pleasant-looking hotel designed in the Persian style with huge arches and high chandeliers. It was a capsule of time recreated in the modern era. Plush Arabian carpets covered the floors and the pleasant smell of shisha and bakhoor an Arabian incense famous for its invigorating properties filled the air. The bellboy carried Sam's belongings to the room while Abdul gave him his visiting card and asked him to call him in case he needed anything. With a broad smile, he turned and left only to come back, "oh I forgot to tell you please don't pay for anything at the hotel, it's on the company just ask them to put it on the tab".

Sam settled into the room and peered outside the window to admire the Arabian Sea and the Corniche below, a beautiful sight to behold.

The next day Sam drove over to the office and was ushered into the meeting room where Mr. Arif awaited him. "Wonderful to have you here," said Arif shaking Sam's hands. "I'm happy you could join us on such short notice". Arif if was a short man with curly black hair, he wore a kandura – and Arabian traditional dress with a black pair of shoes. His face was tanned by the sun and scratch marks covered his left hand. "Falcon, they're my passion," he said looking at his hands. "The young ones scratch your hands. I'm off tomorrow to the desert why don't you join me"?

Chapter Seventeen

The trip to the desert was the start of a wonderful professional relationship between Sam and Arif, who went on to support and mentor Sam. He set up a new software development division and handed Sam the reins of it and offered him a 20% partnership on the software he developed.

Sam thrived in a cohesive and electrifying environment. The place was conducive for learning and development. The office was void of politicking, backbiting, and self-promotion instead, there was a brotherhood unlike any.

When Sam thought he was in heaven it got one step better when he met Adriana. She was recruited to head this testing department. It was love at first sight, Sam resisted the pull fresh out of a sore relationship but it was in vain as he fell head over heels and was pleasantly surprised to learn Adriana felt the same about him.

The two spent the evenings together discussing their life goals and how they seem to have intertwined. Six months down the line they were happily married and had bought a new car and put the down payment for a new house. To their surprise, Arif's brother owned the contracting company and was gave them a hefty discount and a fully furnished house. Sam was living his dream, everything he touched turned to gold.

Chapter Eighteen

Sam returned home one day to find Adrian out to the supermarket. As he walked into the bedroom a dark figure stood in the middle of the room, shocked Sam stepped back as he had not seen it since Kuala Lumpur. Sam was living his dream and had forgotten about his experience with the entity. The figure pointed to the ring and Sam reluctantly removed it and placed it in the hands of the dark figure as it was dissipating Sam gathered the courage, "why me, why did you help me"? The dark figure reformed and a gruff voice answered. "Why were you going to end your life"? "I had no reason to live, all I had worked for all my life was lost and I had no hope of rising back up," said Sam "What led to the situation"? "I used to live with my girlfriend Carol in Thailand where I was working on a project. She started many companies but by the end of last year, none of them did well and she was in great financial difficulty. I stuck my neck out for her by funding her projects and paying her dues by selling my house and car. But due to a financial crisis, my employer was unable to pay my salary for eight months. It was a double whammy as I had sold everything I had to help Carol and now my salary was not coming through. So I was forced to live off my credit card."

"I had helped my brother's family for years financially but in the time of need he turned me down. My friends who promised to help me cut me off and Carol moved away when there was nothing more that I could offer. Despite helping everyone in my time of need everyone deserted me. I had no hope or faith in humanity left to carry on". The cloaked figure answered "this is called transference of karma when you help someone undeservingly your interference in the workings of karma. I tried to stop you by stalling your car when you were about to sell your house, I tried to warn you through your colleague, who told you not to sell your car and take the loans on your credit card. I even delayed your loan application when you tried to take over Carol's loans but you were adamant and came in the line of destiny".

"You took over Carol's karmic dept created due to her irresponsible actions, wherein she did not appreciate what was given to her. Now you are living her life and she is free from her karmic bonds. Transference of karma is as old as the universe sages transferred bad karma of their disciples onto themselves and bore the consequences of it, unfortunately, you have been a victim of your good deeds".

"However, your selfless acts had gained you a lot of good karma which was given to you over the last six months. You have received all that you had lost a car, house, job, salary, respect in society, and most importantly Adriana. A partner who will stand by you as you have for others. Now that the balance of karma has been restored you must lead a life on your terms". "Thank you" said Sam "but who are you"?

-End-

www.ingramcontent.com/pod-product-compliance
Lightning Source LLC
Chambersburg PA
CBHW061447160726
47995CB00003B/1077